MY LIFE
IN DIAGRAMS

First published in the United Kingdom in 2016 by
Portico
1 Gower Street
London
WC1E 6HD

An imprint of Pavilion Books Company Ltd

ISBN 978-1-911042-52-5

A CIP catalogue record for this book is available from the British Library.

10 9 8 7 6 5 4 3 2 1

Illustrations by Pedro Demetriou
Written by Chrissy Williams
Design by Smart Design Studio

Reproduction by Mission Productions Ltd, Hong Kong
Printed and bound by 1010 Printing International Ltd, China

This book can be ordered direct from the publisher at www.pavilionbooks.com

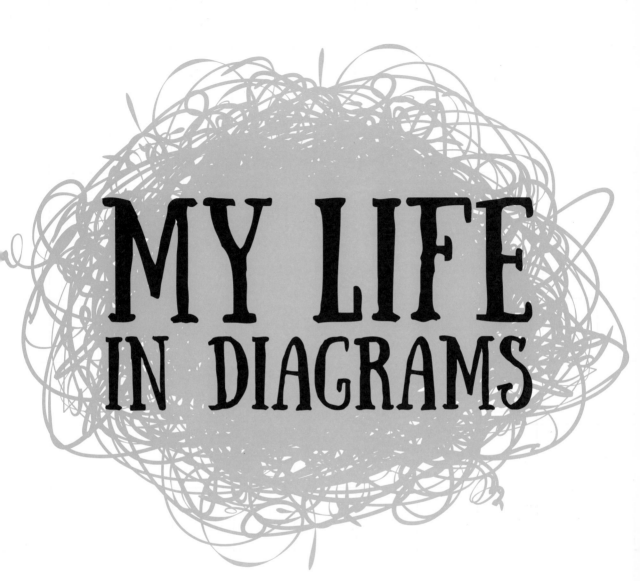

MY LIFE
IN DIAGRAMS

PORTICO

BREAKFAST LOG

	1	2	3	4	5	6	7	8	9	10	11	12	13	14
CORNFLAKES														
TOAST														
LAST NIGHT'S PIZZA														
OATMEAL														
CRISPS														
BACON, EGGS CHIPS, BEANS														
ENERGY BAR														
MUFFINS														
PANCAKES														
NOVELTY CEREAL														
CHOCOLATE BAR														
OTHER														

DAYS

FAVOURITE BREAKFAST

HEALTHY BREAKFAST

THIS IS WHAT I SHOULD EAT FOR BREAKFAST!

Yum!

WRITE IN THE FOODS YOU HAVE EATEN FOR BREAKFAST — HOW MANY ARE IN THE MIDDLE?

WHAT HAVE I EATEN? HOW MANY TIMES HAVE I SKIPPED BREAKFAST?
FILL IN AS MANY BLOCKS AS APPROPRIATE.

| 15 | 16 | 17 | 18 | 19 | 20 | 21 | 22 | 23 | 24 | 25 | 26 | 27 | 28 | 29 | 30 | 31 |

SUMMARY

NUMBER OF TIMES I SKIPPED BREAKFAST ———————————— □

NUMBER OF TIMES I ATE JUNK FOR BREAKFAST ———————————— □

NUMBER OF TIMES I ATE A HEALTHY BREAKFAST ———————————— □

NUMBER OF TIMES I OVERATE AT BREAKFAST ———————————— □

LUNCH LOG

	1	2	3	4	5	6	7	8	9	10	11	12	13	14
SANDWICH TICK HERE IF IT FILLED YOU UP														
SOUP TICK HERE IF IT FILLED YOU UP														
SALAD TICK HERE IF IT FILLED YOU UP														
BURGER TICK HERE IF IT FILLED YOU UP														
BURRITO TICK HERE IF IT FILLED YOU UP														
OTHER TICK HERE IF IT FILLED YOU UP														

DAYS

WHAT'S IN YOUR FAVOURITE LUNCH?
DESIGN YOUR IDEAL LUNCH FROM THE FOLLOWING INGREDIENTS

CHICKEN ☐	TUNA ☐	RICE ☐
BEEF ☐	VEGGIE MEAT ☐	CHOCOLATE ☐
PORK ☐	GREEN SALAD ☐	NOODLES ☐
BACON ☐	TOMATOES ☐	PASTA ☐
HAM ☐	CHEESE ☐	BREAD ☐

MY IDEAL LUNCH IS A ....

WHAT'S FOR LUNCH - SOMETHING FILLING AND DELICIOUS?
FILL IN AS MANY BLOCKS AS APPROPRIATE.

| 15 | 16 | 17 | 18 | 19 | 20 | 21 | 22 | 23 | 24 | 25 | 26 | 27 | 28 | 29 | 30 | 31 |

SUMMARY

MOST POPULAR LUNCH ....

LEAST POPULAR LUNCH ....

MOST FILLING LUNCH ....

LEAST FILLING LUNCH ....

DINNER LOG

HOME-MADE														
RESTAURANT														
DELIVERY														
DAYS	1	2	3	4	5	6	7	8	9	10	11	12	13	14

GUILTY PLEASURES

APPETISERS
WRITE DOWN YOUR MOST FAVOURITE APPETISERS

GUILTY PLEASURES

MAINS
WRITE DOWN YOUR MOST FAVOURITE MAINS

KEEP TRACK OF HOW AND WHERE YOU EAT! BE HONEST, NOW...

15	16	17	18	19	20	21	22	23	24	25	26	27	28	29	30	31

DESSERTS
WRITE DOWN YOUR MOST FAVOURITE DESSERTS

GUILTY PLEASURES

SUMMARY

NUMBER OF HOME-MADE MEALS ....

NUMBER OF RESTAURANT MEALS ....

NUMBER OF MEALS DELIVERED ....

AMOUNT OF GUILT YOU FEEL ....

YOUR IDEAL DINNER ....
(I.E. THE FAVOURITE FROM EACH OF YOUR
APPETISERS, MAINS AND DESSERTS LISTS)

FIVE-A-DAY TRACKER

	1	2	3	4	5	6	7	8	9	10
5										
4										
3										
2										
1										

DAYS

	11	12	13	14	15	16	17	18	19	20
5										
4										
3										
2										
1										

DAYS

	21	22	23	24	25	26	27	28	29	30	31
5											
4											
3											
2											
1											

DAYS

MAKE SURE YOU'RE GETTING ENOUGH OF YOUR FIVE-A-DAY FRUIT AND VEGETABLES!

WHAT DOES "ONE" OF YOUR FIVE-A-DAY LOOK LIKE?

1 X WHOLE FRUIT (MEDIUM-SIZED, LIKE APPLES, BANANAS, PEARS, ETC),
1 X WHOLE VEGETABLE (MEDIUM-SIZED, LIKE ONIONS, ETC),
1 X BOWL (OF GREEN SALADS ETC), 1 X GLASS (OF PURE FRUIT JUICE),
3 X HEAPED TABLESPOONS (OF BOTH GREEN AND ROOT VEG, LIKE CABBAGE, CARROTS, ETC)

FILL IN THIS BARCHART USING THE INFORMATION ON THE OPPOSITE PAGE.

HOW MANY IN A MONTH					
OVER 20					
10-20					
5-10					
1-5					

NAME OF MONTH

SUMMARY

TYPE OF FRUIT EATEN THE MOST OFTEN ....

TYPE OF VEG EATEN THE MOST OFTEN ....

TYPE OF FRUIT/VEG I REALLY NEED TO EAT MORE OF ....

TYPE OF FRUIT/VEG I ABSOLUTELY REFUSE TO EAT ....

SNACKING ISN'T ALWAYS A BAD THING — YOU NEED TO KEEP YOUR ENERGY UP!
USE THIS PAGE TO TRACK WHAT YOU SNACK!

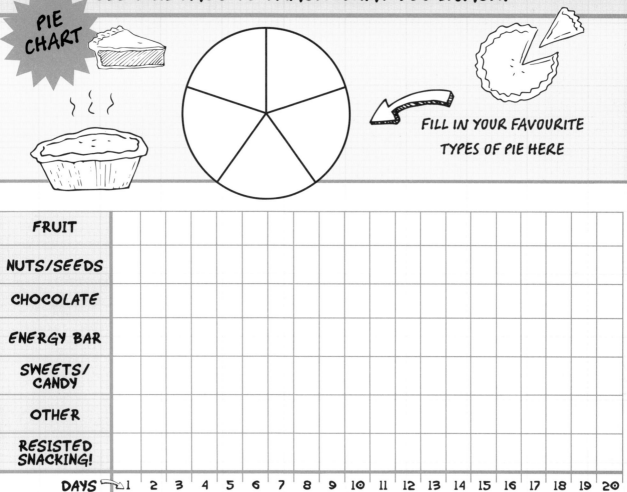

PIE CHART

FILL IN YOUR FAVOURITE TYPES OF PIE HERE

	1	2	3	4	5	6	7	8	9	10	11	12	13	14	15	16	17	18	19	20
FRUIT																				
NUTS/SEEDS																				
CHOCOLATE																				
ENERGY BAR																				
SWEETS/CANDY																				
OTHER																				
RESISTED SNACKING!																				

DAYS

SUMMARY

SNACK I ATE THE MOST ....

SNACK I HATE THE MOST ....

SNACK I SHOULD EAT MORE OF ....

NUMBER OF TIMES I RESISTED SNACKING ....

BROADER FOOD HORIZONS...

AFRICAN
BOBOTIE ☐
CROCODILE ☐
OSTRICH ☐
OR SOMETHING ELSE MAYBE?

AMERICAN
BURGER ☐
SOUL FOOD ☐
TWINKIES ☐
OR SOMETHING ELSE MAYBE?

BRITISH
FISH AND CHIPS ☐
BEEF WELLINGTON ☐
FULL ENGLISH BREAKFAST ☐
OR SOMETHING ELSE MAYBE?

CARIBBEAN
JERK CHICKEN ☐
GOAT CURRY ☐
SALTFISH AND ACKEE ☐
OR SOMETHING ELSE MAYBE?

CHINESE
SICHUAN BEEF ☐
CHILLI CRAB ☐
PEKING DUMPLINGS ☐
OR SOMETHING ELSE MAYBE?

EAST EUROPEAN
GOULASH ☐
BORSCHT ☐
PIEROGI ☐
OR SOMETHING ELSE MAYBE?

FRENCH
MOULES FRITES ☐
CASSOULET ☐
SALADE NIÇOISE ☐
OR SOMETHING ELSE MAYBE?

GREEK
LAMB SKEWERS ☐
MOUSSAKA ☐
HALLOUMI SAGANAKI ☐
OR SOMETHING ELSE MAYBE?

INDIAN
CURRIES ☐
DAAL ☐
CARDAMOM KULFI ☐
OR SOMETHING ELSE MAYBE?

IRISH
IRISH STEW ☐
COLCANNON ☐
BARMBRACK ☐
OR SOMETHING ELSE MAYBE?

ITALIAN
LASAGNE ☐
RISOTTO ☐
GNOCCHI ☐
OR SOMETHING ELSE MAYBE?

JAPANESE
SUSHI ☐
TEMPURA ☐
TERIYAKI ☐
OR SOMETHING ELSE MAYBE?

MEXICAN
CHILAQUILES ☐
MOLE SAUCE ☐
TAMALES ☐
OR SOMETHING ELSE MAYBE?

NORDIC
FISH PIE ☐
MUTTON STEW ☐
BALTIC HERRING ☐
OR SOMETHING ELSE MAYBE?

NORTH AFRICAN
TAGINE ☐
CUSCUS ☐
M'HANNCHA ☐
OR SOMETHING ELSE MAYBE?

HOW ADVENTUROUS ARE MY EATING HABITS?
TICK OFF EACH ONE OF THESE AFTER YOU'VE TRIED THEM!

PORTUGUESE

PIRI-PIRI CHICKEN ☐

CALDO VERDE ☐

CUSTARD TART ☐

OR SOMETHING ELSE MAYBE?

....

SOUTH AMERICAN

CEVICHE ☐

EMPANADAS ☐

CAIPIRINHAS ☐

OR SOMETHING ELSE MAYBE?

....

SPANISH

TAPAS ☐

PAELLA ☐

CHORIZO ☐

OR SOMETHING ELSE MAYBE?

....

THAI AND SOUTHEAST ASIA

GREEN CURRY ☐

AYAM SIOH ☐

BÁNH CHƯNG ☐

OR SOMETHING ELSE MAYBE?

....

TURKISH AND MIDDLE EASTERN

TABBOULEH ☐

BABA GANOUSH ☐

BAKLAVA ☐

OR SOMETHING ELSE MAYBE?

....

SUMMARY

MY FAVOURITE CUISINE IS ....

MY FAVOURITE DISH IS ....

I AM SLIGHTLY INTIMIDATED BY ....

I REALLY NEED TO TRY ....

YOU ARE WHAT YOU DRINK

THE EATWELL GUIDE SAYS WE SHOULD ALL DRINK 6-8 GLASSES OF WATER EVERY DAY.
FILL IN THE BLOCKS ON THIS CHART TO TRACK YOURS.

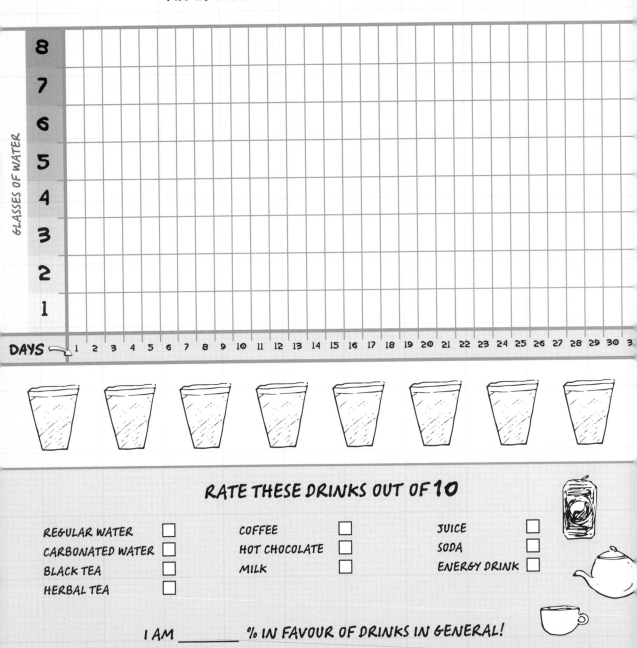

GLASSES OF WATER

8
7
6
5
4
3
2
1

DAYS → 1 2 3 4 5 6 7 8 9 10 11 12 13 14 15 16 17 18 19 20 21 22 23 24 25 26 27 28 29 30 3.

RATE THESE DRINKS OUT OF 10

REGULAR WATER ☐   COFFEE ☐   JUICE ☐
CARBONATED WATER ☐   HOT CHOCOLATE ☐   SODA ☐
BLACK TEA ☐   MILK ☐   ENERGY DRINK ☐
HERBAL TEA ☐

I AM _____ % IN FAVOUR OF DRINKS IN GENERAL!

OUR BODIES ARE ABOUT 60% WATER, WHICH WE LOSE ON A DAILY BASIS. USE THIS PAGE TO TRACK WHAT YOU PUT BACK IN!

FILL IN YOUR FAVOURITE DRINKS BELOW AND USE THIS CHART
TO TICK OFF EACH DAY YOU HAD ONE.

DAYS DRUNK

	MONDAY	TUESDAY	WEDNESDAY	THURSDAY	FRIDAY	SATURDAY	SUNDAY
FRUIT PUNCH							
....							
....							
....							
....							
....							
....							

SUMMARY

NUMBER OF DAYS I DRANK MY 6-8 GLASSES ....

MY FAVOURITE DRINK (BY PERCENTAGE) ....

DRINK I HAVE MOST FREQUENTLY ....

DRINK I REALLY NEED TO CUT DOWN ON ....

FITNESS

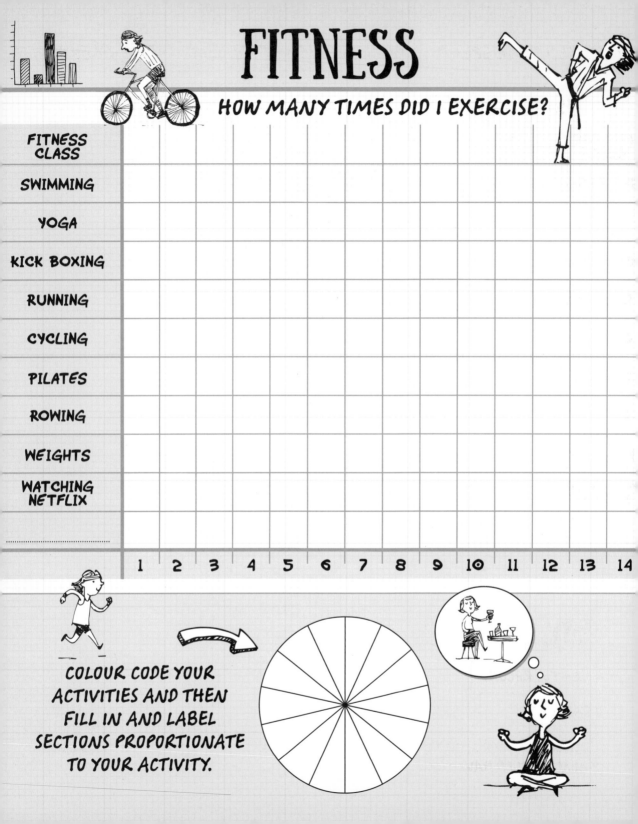

HOW MANY TIMES DID I EXERCISE?

	1	2	3	4	5	6	7	8	9	10	11	12	13	14
FITNESS CLASS														
SWIMMING														
YOGA														
KICK BOXING														
RUNNING														
CYCLING														
PILATES														
ROWING														
WEIGHTS														
WATCHING NETFLIX														

COLOUR CODE YOUR ACTIVITIES AND THEN FILL IN AND LABEL SECTIONS PROPORTIONATE TO YOUR ACTIVITY.

HOW MANY TIMES HAVE I BEEN A COUCH POTATO?

	1	2	3	4	5	6	7	8	9	10	11	12	13	14
FITNESS CLASS														
SWIMMING														
YOGA														
KICK BOXING														
RUNNING														
CYCLING														
PILATES														
ROWING														
WEIGHTS														
WATCHING NETFLIX														

SUMMARY

I WENT A RECORD [   ] DAYS WITHOUT EXERCISING

I EXERCISED [   ] MANY DAYS IN A ROW

I SAT ON MY BUM AND WATCHED NETFLIX [   ] TIMES
WHEN I SHOULD HAVE BEEN GETTING FIT

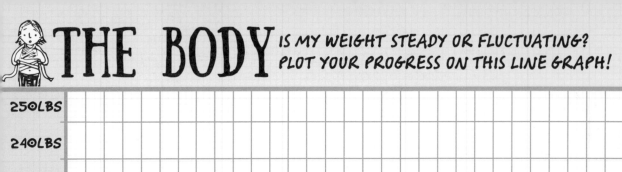

250LBS

240LBS

230LBS

220LBS

210LBS

200LBS

190LBS

180LBS

170LBS

160LBS

150LBS

140LBS

130LBS

120LBS

110LBS

100LBS

90LBS

80LBS

70LBS

DAYS 1 2 3 4 5 6 7 8 9 10 11 12 13 14 15 16 17 18 19 20 21 22 23 24 25 26 27 28 29 30 3

FILL IN THESE BLANKS WITH AVERAGE CALORIE COUNTS OF THE FOOD YOU EAT MOST OFTEN.

MEDIUM-SIZED BANANA APPROX 105 CALORIES .... / .... CALORIES

SNICKERS BAR APPROX 488 CALORIES .... / .... CALORIES

SLICE OF CHEESECAKE APPROX 257 CALORIES .... / .... CALORIES

TO BURN ROUGHLY 100 CALORIES YOU NEED TO...

SWIM FOR 8 MINS

JOG FOR 11 MINS

CYCLE FOR 15 MINS

OR WALK FOR 28 MINS

CALORIE COUNTING

MOST FOODS HAVE THEIR CALORIE COUNT LISTED ON THE PACKAGING THESE DAYS — USE THIS TO RECORD YOUR CALORIE INTAKE EVERY DAY

	MONDAY	TUESDAY	WEDNESDAY	THURSDAY	FRIDAY	SATURDAY	SUNDAY
BREAKFAST							
LUNCH							
DINNER							
SNACKS							
TOTAL							

SWEET DREAMS

FILL IN A BLOCK FOR EVERY HOUR YOU SLEPT,
THEN WRITE YOUR TOTAL HOURS AT THE BOTTOM.

DAYS	1	2	3	4	5	6	7	8	9	10	11	12	13	14
9PM														
10PM														
11PM														
12AM														
1AM														
2AM														
3AM														
4AM														
5AM														
6AM														
7AM														
8AM														
9AM														
10AM														
11AM														
TOTAL														

WEB MD SAYS MOST ADULTS NEED 7-9 HOURS SLEEP DAILY. I LIKE TO GET 10 HOURS SLEEP A DAY, PLUS WHATEVER I CAN GET AT NIGHT.

WE ARE SUCH STUFF AS DREAMS ARE MADE OF — SO KEEP YOUR SLEEP IN CHECK ON THIS PAGE!

PUT A TICK IN THE BOX WHEN THIS DREAM OCCURS
AND SEE WHAT YOU DREAM ABOUT THE MOST!

BORING NONSENSE	MONEY	BEING TRAPPED	HOUSE	FOOD	WATER	FALLING	BEING CHASED	FLYING	
									ME
									FAMILY MEMBER
									FRIEND
									PET
									AUTHORITY FIGURE
									WINGED CREATURE
									CAN'T REMEMBER

SUMMARY

TO WORK OUT THE AVERAGE AMOUNT OF SLEEP
YOU GET EVERY NIGHT, ADD UP THE TOTALS OF THE
14 NIGHTS ABOVE, THEN DIVIDE THAT TOTAL BY 14.

I REALLY SHOULD TRY TO GET MORE/LESS* SLEEP. (DELETE AS APPROPRIATE.)

STRESSED OUT

LOOK AT THE NEXT PAGE FOR SOME USEFUL TIPS ON HOW TO COMBAT THE PHYSICAL SYMPTOMS OF STRESS.

WE ALL GET STRESSED OUT ON A DAILY BASIS. USE THIS PAGE TO FIGURE OUT WHAT STRESSES YOU OUT THE MOST, AND THINK ABOUT HOW TO FIX IT.

	1	2	3	4	5	6	7	8	9	10	11	12	13	14	15	16	17	18	19	20
WORK																				
TOO MUCH TO DO																				
PEOPLE PROBLEMS																				
FACING DISCRIMINATION																				
FEELING INSECURE																				
LIFE																				
RELATIONSHIP TROUBLE																				
HOUSE PROBLEMS																				
MONEY WORRIES																				
ILLNESS																				
FAMILY																				
BEREAVEMENT																				
OTHER TRAUMA																				

DAYS ➜

ASSIGN A COLOUR TO EACH OF THE FOLLOWING — THEN FILL IN THE CHART EVERY DAY, AND TRY TO ASSIGN ONE OF THE FOLLOWING UNDERLYING CAUSES BEHIND EACH INSTANCE OF STRESS.

FEAR / UNCERTAINTY ☐   NEGATIVE ATTITUDE ☐   LACK OF SUPPORT ☐
UNREALISTIC EXPECTATIONS ☐   LACK OF CONTROL ☐   FEELINGS OF LOSS ☐

SUMMARY

THE BIGGEST SOURCE OF STRESS FOR ME IS ....

.... IS BEHIND THE MAJORITY OF MY STRESS.

WEB.MD HAS SOME USEFUL TIPS ON REDUCING STRESS. ASSIGN EACH ONE A COLOUR, THEN FILL IN THIS GLASS EACH TIME YOU USE ONE, UNTIL YOUR GLASS IS MORE THAN HALF-FULL!

ALLOW YOURSELF TO ASK FOR HELP IF YOU NEED IT. ☐

TAKE A BREAK IF YOU'RE FEELING STRESSED. ☐

TRY TO BE POSITIVE – REMEMBER YOU'RE DOING YOUR BEST. ☐

DO SOMETHING RELAXING FOR AT LEAST 20 MINUTES A DAY. ☐

TOP TIPS FOR GENERAL STRESSBUSTING

- EAT HEALTHY BALANCED MEALS.
- GET ENOUGH REST AND SLEEP.
- GET REGULAR EXERCISE.
- DRINK ENOUGH WATER.
- STROKE A DOG. ANY DOG.

HOW HAPPY IS YOUR HOME?

	BEDROOM	BATHROOM	KITCHEN	LIVING ROOM	OTHER
KEEP THE FLOOR CLEAR					
DISPLAY SENTIMENTAL THINGS					
DE-CLUTTER AT LEAST ONE SURFACE					
ADD A GREEN PLANT OR FLOWERS					
OPEN WINDOWS DAILY FOR FRESH AIR					

RELAX!

THE ONLY THING BETTER THAN RELAXATION IS ORGANISED RELAXATION! OKAY, THAT MAY NOT ACTUALLY BE TRUE, BUT HERE'S A WAY FOR YOU TO MAKE THE BEST USE OF THE SPACE IN YOUR HOUSE.

	BEDROOM	BATHROOM	KITCHEN	LIVING ROOM	OTHER
MEDITATION					
READING A BOOK					
SNOOZING					
....					

THE SMALLEST THINGS CAN MAKE YOUR HOUSE FEEL MORE LIKE A HOME...

THANKFULNESS JOURNAL

IT CAN BE USEFUL TO WRITE DOWN THINGS YOU'RE THANKFUL FOR AT THE END OF EACH DAY — FOCUS ON THE GOOD STUFF. MAKE A LIST OF THINGS YOU'RE THANKFUL FOR BELOW.

MOTIVATIONAL NOTES

WOULDN'T IT BE NICE IF YOU COULD KEEP THAT HAPPINESS GOING IN THE MORNING? USE THIS SPACE TO WRITE YOURSELF SOME MOTIVATIONAL MESSAGES TO READ IN THE MORNINGS.

LAUGHTER IS THE BEST MEDICINE

THE INTERNET IS OUR FRIEND WHEN IT COMES TO LAUGHTER —
— HOW MANY TIMES HAVE YOU LAUGHED AT THESE TODAY?

TALKING DOGS ☐   GIGGLING BABIES ☐   CATS IN HATS ☐
DANCING SHEEP ☐   GOATS IN COATS ☐

A GREENER HOME

IT CAN BE EASIER THAN YOU THINK TO HAVE A GREENER HOME — AND THE FIRST STEP IS FIGURING OUT WHAT AREAS YOU NEED TO CUT DOWN ON.

USE A PALE COLOUR TO FILL OUT THIS BAR CHART AND FIGURE OUT HOW LONG YOU LEAVE YOUR APPLIANCES PLUGGED IN FOR. THEN, USE A DARKER COLOUR TO FILL OVER HOW LONG YOU ACTUALLY NEED TO LEAVE THEM PLUGGED IN FOR.

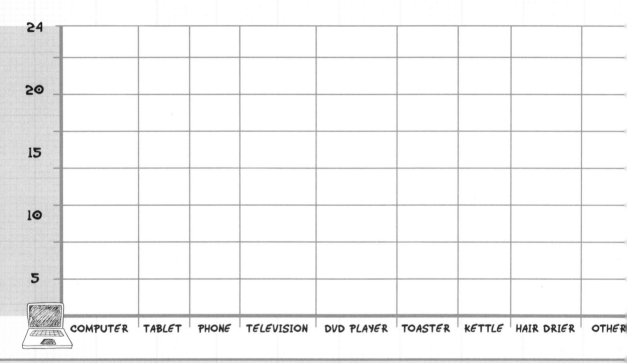

24								
20								
15								
10								
5								
COMPUTER	TABLET	PHONE	TELEVISION	DVD PLAYER	TOASTER	KETTLE	HAIR DRIER	OTHER

FILL IN THIS DIAGRAM AS YOU THINK BEST.

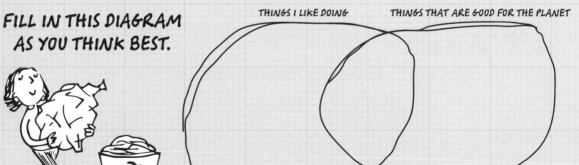

THINGS I LIKE DOING   THINGS THAT ARE GOOD FOR THE PLANET

DO THESE THINGS MORE!

HERE'S A FEW EASY WAYS TO MAKE YOUR HOUSE GREENER!

DONE IT!

TRADE IN YOUR LIGHTBULBS FOR CFL / LOW ENERGY BULBS! ☐

UNPLUG APPLIANCES WHEN YOU'RE NOT USING THEM! ☐

KEEP YOUR BLINDS OPEN TO WARM THE HOUSE FASTER! ☐

INVITE FRIENDS OVER IN WINTER TO MAKE THE HOUSE WARMER! ☐

DECIDE WHAT YOU WANT BEFORE HOLDING THE FRIDGE DOOR OPEN FOR AGES WHILE CHOOSING! ☐

USE ECO-SCENTS INSTEAD OF SYNTHETIC AIR FRESHENERS! ☐

GROW HOUSEPLANTS TO IMPROVE YOUR AIR QUALITY! ☐

WASH YOUR CLOTHES AT A LOWER TEMPERATURE! ☐

TURN OFF THE TAP WHILE YOU BRUSH YOUR TEETH! ☐

HAVE SHOWERS INSTEAD OF BATHS! ☐

TAKE OLD CLOTHES TO LOCAL CHARITY SHOPS! ☐

GIVE MONEY TO CHARITY! ☐

.... ☐

.... ☐

SUMMARY

THE EASIEST WAY FOR ME TO MAKE MY HOUSE GREENER IS

....

THE AREA I NEED TO MAKE THE MOST EFFORT IN IS PROBABLY

....

SEE THE WORLD!

SHADE IN ALL THE PLACES YOU'VE BEEN TO. USE NUMBERS TO ADD PLACES YOU'D LIKE TO VISIT, IN ORDER OF HOW MUCH YOU WANT TO VISIT THEM.

L.A.

NEW YORK

MEXICO CITY

RIO DE JANEIRO

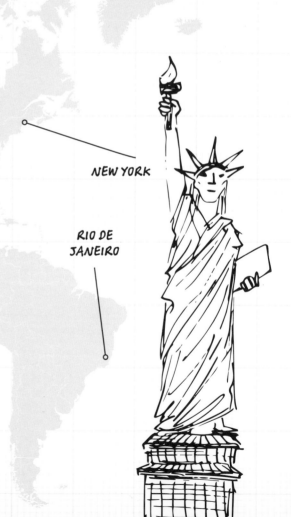

THE WORLD'S YOUR OYSTER! MARK OFF EVERYWHERE YOU'VE BEEN ON THIS MAP, AND EVERYWHERE YOU WANT TO GO!

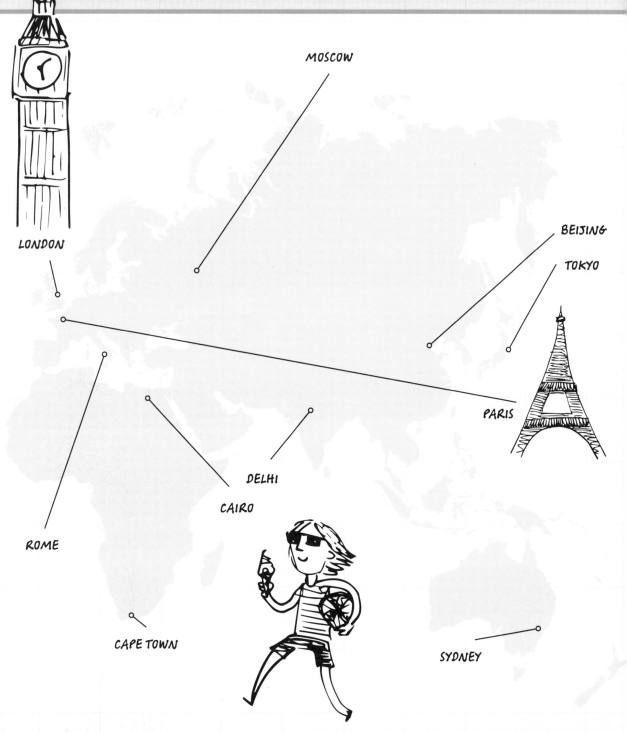

HOLIDAY TIME!

USE THIS VENN DIAGRAM TO FIGURE OUT WHERE YOU WANT TO GO. CROSS OUT THE LABELS YOU DON'T WANT UNTIL THERE'S ONLY ONE LEFT IN EACH CIRCLE, THEN FILL IN THE CENTRE OF THE DIAGRAM WITH THE PLACE YOU THINK BEST MATCHES ALL THOSE REQUIREMENTS!

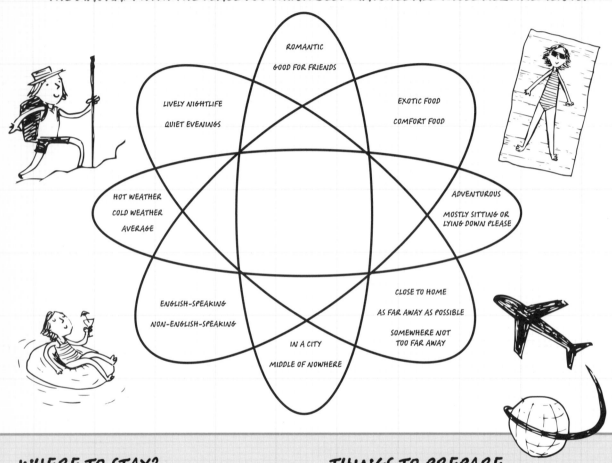

ROMANTIC

GOOD FOR FRIENDS

LIVELY NIGHTLIFE

QUIET EVENINGS

EXOTIC FOOD

COMFORT FOOD

HOT WEATHER

COLD WEATHER

AVERAGE

ADVENTUROUS

MOSTLY SITTING OR LYING DOWN PLEASE

ENGLISH-SPEAKING

NON-ENGLISH-SPEAKING

CLOSE TO HOME

AS FAR AWAY AS POSSIBLE

SOMEWHERE NOT TOO FAR AWAY

IN A CITY

MIDDLE OF NOWHERE

WHERE TO STAY?

- GET RECOMMENDATIONS FROM FRIENDS ☐
- READ REVIEWS ON TRAVEL WEBSITES ☐
  (LIKE TRIPADVISOR)
- SHOP AROUND TO GET THE BEST DEAL ☐
- BOOK AS EARLY AS POSSIBLE ☐

THINGS TO PREPARE

- PLAN YOUR TRAVEL, FROM YOUR
  FRONT DOOR TO THE OTHER END ☐
- BUY TICKETS IN ADVANCE FOR
  THE BEST DEALS ☐
- DO YOU NEED A PASSPORT? ☐
- DO YOU NEED TO GET A VISA? ☐
- DO YOU NEED TO HAVE INJECTIONS? ☐
- DO YOU NEED FOREIGN MONEY? ☐

MY NORMAL DAYS

BREAKFAST AT .... O'CLOCK,
CONSISTING OF ....
....
....
....

LUNCH AT .... O'CLOCK,
CONSISTING OF ....
....
....
....

DINNER AT .... O'CLOCK,
CONSISTING OF ....
....
....
....

SLEEP AT ...., DREAMING ABOUT
....
....
....
....

MY PERFECT HOLIDAY DAY

BREAKFAST AT .... O'CLOCK,
CONSISTING OF ....
....
....
....

LUNCH AT .... O'CLOCK,
CONSISTING OF ....
....
....
....

DINNER AT .... O'CLOCK,
CCONSISTING OF ....
....
....
....

SLEEP AT ...., DREAMING ABOUT
....
....
....
....

CHORES A PLENTY

THE GREAT AND POWERFUL OZ

WHITE WIZARD

WITCHES AND WARLOCKS

MASTER OF SPELLS

SORCEROR'S APPRENTICE

WITCH'S FAMILIAR

31 30 29 28 27 26 25 24 23 22 21 20 19 18 17 16 15 14 13 12 11 10 9 8 7 6 5 4 3 2 1

| MAKE BEDS | WASH DISHES | URGENT LAUNDRY | WASH KITCHEN COUNTERS |

CHORES AT HOME CAN SEEM LIKE THEY DRAG ON ENDLESSLY, BUT SOME STUDIES SUGGEST YOU ACTUALLY ENJOY DOING THEM MORE IF YOU GAMIFY THEM AND REWARD YOURSELF! SO...

	WEEK 1	WEEK 2	WEEK 3	WEEK 4	WEEK 5	WEEK 6	WEEK 7
WATER PLANTS							
PUT OUT BINS							
PUT OUT RECYCLING							
CLEAN BATHROOM							
CLEAN FLOORS							
CLEAN TOWELS							
CLEAN BEDSHEETS							
DO SOME DUSTING							
CLEAN OUT FRIDGE							

WRITE DOWN SOME SONGS IT'S GOOD TO PUT ON WHILE DOING CHORES

GEORGE FORMBY 'WHEN I'M CLEANING WINDOWS'

SUMMARY

CHORE I ENJOY MOST ....

CHORE I HATE MOST ....

CHORE I AM BEST AT ....

REWARD FOR DOING MY CHORES ....

STAYING ON TOP OF YOUR BILLS

UTILITIES

	DATE LAST PAID	AMOUNT	APPROX AMOUNT PER YEAR	DATE NEXT BILL DUE	DATE NEXT BILL DUE
GAS					
ELECTRIC					
WATER					
OTHER LOCAL / COUNCIL TAX					

TOTAL AMOUNT PER YEAR

MONTHLY

	DATE LAST PAID	AMOUNT	APPROX AMOUNT PER YEAR	DATE NEXT BILL DUE	DATE NEXT BILL DUE
PHONE					
LOAN REPAYMENTS					
CREDIT/STORE CARDS					
REGULAR TRAVEL					
REGULAR SPORT					
MEDICAL					
CHARITY					
GROCERIES					
OTHER					

TOTAL AMOUNT PER YEAR

ANNUALLY

	DATE LAST PAID	AMOUNT	APPROX AMOUNT PER YEAR	DATE NEXT BILL DUE	DATE NEXT BILL DUE
INSURANCE					
MEMBERSHIPS					
OTHER					

TOTAL AMOUNT YOU SPEND ON THESE IN TOTAL EACH YEAR

NOW WORK OUT THOSE THREE SETS OF PAYMENTS AS PERCENTAGES SO YOU CAN SEE HOW MUCH YOU SPEND ON WHAT.

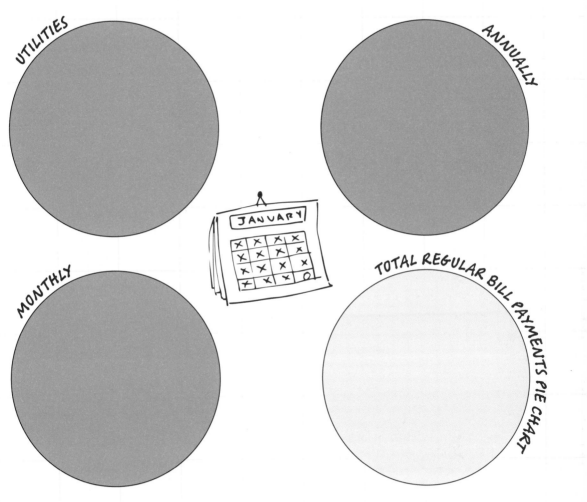

UTILITIES

ANNUALLY

MONTHLY

TOTAL REGULAR BILL PAYMENTS PIE CHART

SUMMARY

AREA I NEED TO TRY AND CUT DOWN ON ....

AREA I NEED TO LOOK FOR BETTER DEALS ON ....

AREA I SHOULD REALLY SPEND MORE ON ....

SPENDING MONEY!

GO THROUGH YOUR LAST BANK STATEMENT AND WRITE DOWN EVERY AMOUNT YOU SPENT UNDER THE FOLLOWING CATEGORIES.

FOOD (EXTRA TO REGULAR GROCERY SHOPPING)	DRINK	SOCIALISING (OTHER)	CLOTHES	BOOKS	GAMES	MUSIC	HOBBIES	GIFTS	SPECIAL TRIPS / HOLIDAY	OTHER

MONTHLY TOTALS

GRAND TOTAL

YOU'VE COVERED ALL THE BORING STUFF YOU HAVE TO SPEND YOUR MONEY ON —
NOW IT'S TIME TO THINK ABOUT THE FUN STUFF YOU WANT TO SPEND YOUR MONEY ON!

FOOD (EXTRA TO REGULAR GROCERY SHOPPING) ☐   MUSIC ☐

DRINK ☐   HOBBIES ☐

SOCIALISING (OTHER) ☐   GIFTS ☐

CLOTHES ☐   SPECIAL TRIPS / HOLIDAY ☐

BOOKS ☐   OTHER ☐

GAMES ☐

ONE POUND

CHOOSE COLOURS FOR EACH CATEGORY, THEN FILL IN THIS PIE CHART TO SHOW HOW MUCH YOU SPEND IN EACH AREA OVERALL.

FILL IN THIS CHART TO SHOW HOW MUCH YOU WANT TO SPEND ON EACH OF THESE CATEGORIES EACH MONTH!

SUMMARY

I SPEND WAY TOO MUCH ON ....

I'M HAPPY WITH THE AMOUNT I SPEND ON ....

I COULD PROBABLY SPEND MORE ON ....

YOU ARE WHAT YOU WEAR

BEST FRIENDS FOREVER

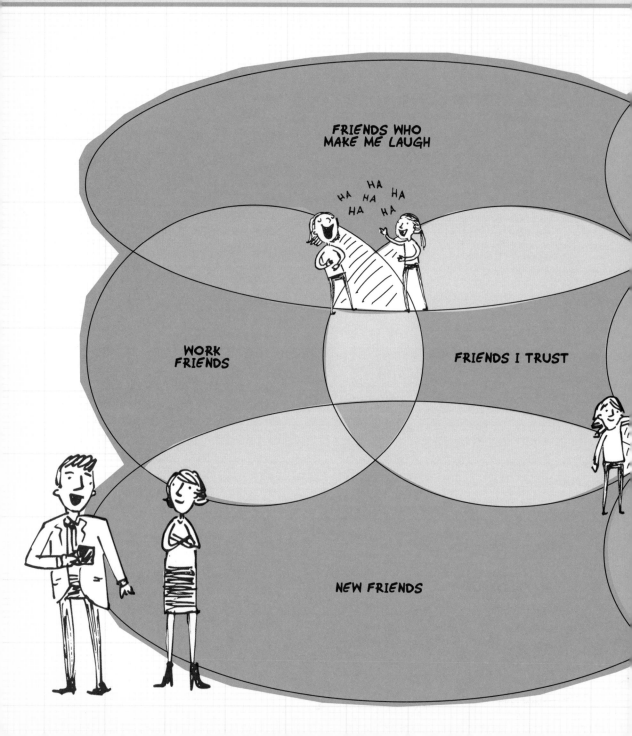

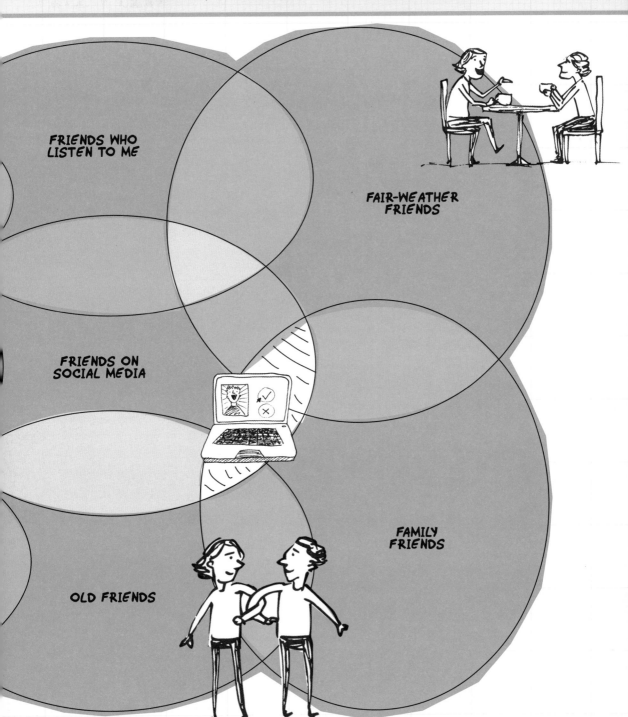

FRIENDS INDEED

FILL THESE IN AND MAKE A DATA FILE FOR EACH OF YOUR CLOSEST FRIENDS.

NAME

AGE

FIRST MET AT

LOVES

HATES

FAVOURITE ACTOR

FAVOURITE FOOD

IDEAL NIGHT OUT

NAME

AGE

FIRST MET AT

LOVES

HATES

FAVOURITE ACTOR

FAVOURITE FOOD

IDEAL NIGHT OUT

NAME

AGE

FIRST MET AT

LOVES

HATES

FAVOURITE ACTOR

FAVOURITE FOOD

IDEAL NIGHT OUT

USE THIS PAGE TO THINK ABOUT WHO YOU SPEND YOUR TIME WITH, WHO YOU WANT TO SPEND YOUR TIME WITH, AND HOW YOU CAN SHOW YOUR FRIENDS YOU CARE.

FFRIENDSHIP GROUP ☐
CLOSE FRIENDS ☐
COLLEAGUES ☐
FAMILY ☐

ASSIGN A COLOUR TO EACH OF THESE GROUPS AND BLOCK OUT THE HOURS A DAY YOU SPEND WITH THOSE PEOPLE (IN PERSON, NOT ONLINE!).

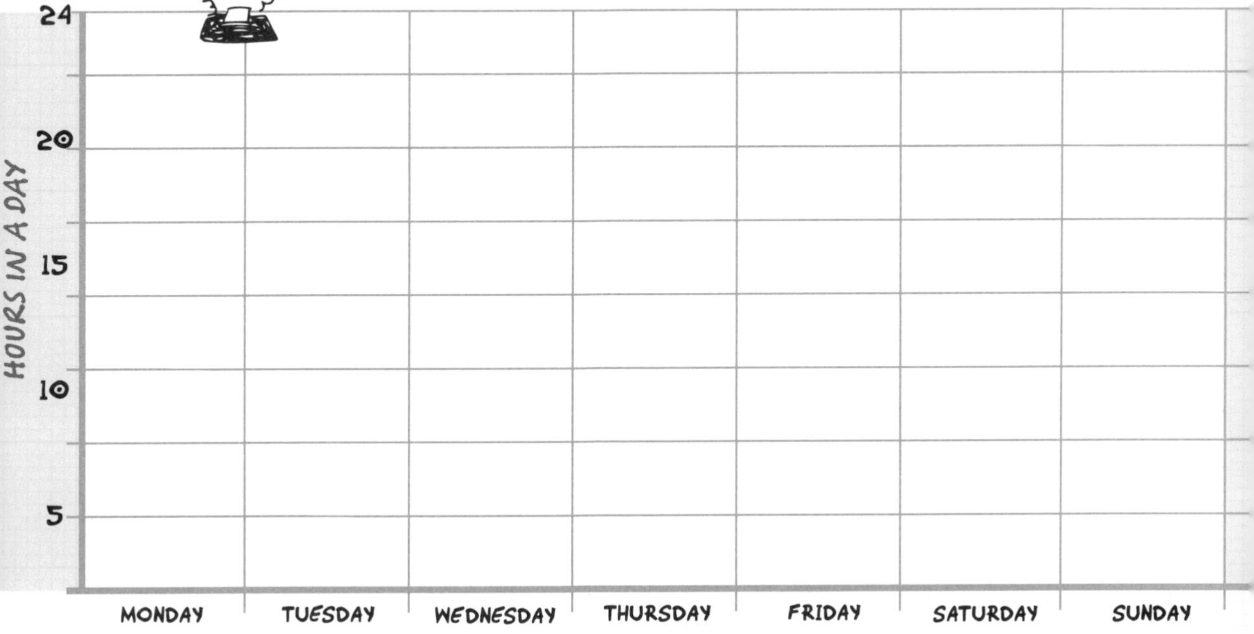

HOURS IN A DAY

24

20

15

10

5

| MONDAY | TUESDAY | WEDNESDAY | THURSDAY | FRIDAY | SATURDAY | SUNDAY |

✗   ✓

SUMMARY

PEOPLE I WANT TO SEE MORE OF ....

PEOPLE I WANT TO SEE LESS OF ....

BIRTHDAY PLANNER

JANUARY

....
....
....
....

FEBRUARY

14 FEB – VALENTINE'S DAY

....
....
....
....

MARCH

17 MAR – ST PATRICK'S DAY

....
....
....
....

JULY

....
....
....
....
....

AUGUST

....
....
....
....
....

SEPTEMBER

....
....
....
....
....

NO EXCUSES FOR FORGETTING FAMILY AND FRIENDS' GIFTS NOW –

EVER MISSED A FRIEND OR FAMILY MEMBER'S IMPORTANT BIRTHDAY? KEEP TRACK OF THEM ALL HERE SO YOU'LL NEVER FORGET THEM AGAIN!

APRIL

MAY

1 MAY – MAY DAY

JUNE

OCTOBER

NOVEMBER

DECEMBER

25 DEC – CHRISTMAS DAY

ADD THEIR BIRTHDAYS IN ABOVE, AND PREPARE YOURSELF FOR THE BUSY MONTHS!

FACING THE FAMILY

START WITH ME, FILL IN THE NAMES ON THIS FAMILY TREE, AND ADD OTHER BRANCHES AS APPROPRIATE.

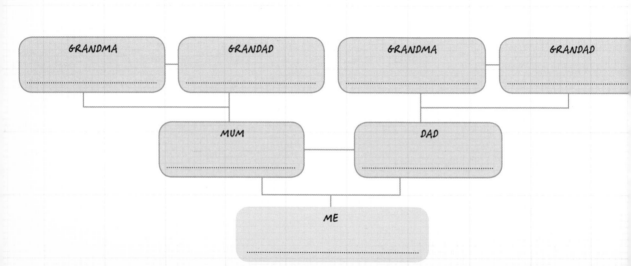

GRANDMA

GRANDAD

GRANDMA

GRANDAD

MUM

DAD

ME

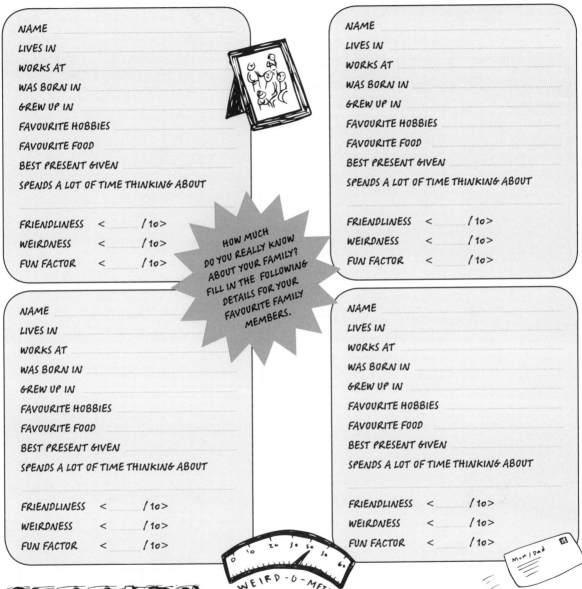

NAME

LIVES IN

WORKS AT

WAS BORN IN

GREW UP IN

FAVOURITE HOBBIES

FAVOURITE FOOD

BEST PRESENT GIVEN

SPENDS A LOT OF TIME THINKING ABOUT

FRIENDLINESS   < ...... / 10 >

WEIRDNESS   < ...... / 10 >

FUN FACTOR   < ...... / 10 >

NAME

LIVES IN

WORKS AT

WAS BORN IN

GREW UP IN

FAVOURITE HOBBIES

FAVOURITE FOOD

BEST PRESENT GIVEN

SPENDS A LOT OF TIME THINKING ABOUT

FRIENDLINESS   < ...... / 10 >

WEIRDNESS   < ...... / 10 >

FUN FACTOR   < ...... / 10 >

HOW MUCH DO YOU REALLY KNOW ABOUT YOUR FAMILY? FILL IN THE FOLLOWING DETAILS FOR YOUR FAVOURITE FAMILY MEMBERS.

NAME

LIVES IN

WORKS AT

WAS BORN IN

GREW UP IN

FAVOURITE HOBBIES

FAVOURITE FOOD

BEST PRESENT GIVEN

SPENDS A LOT OF TIME THINKING ABOUT

FRIENDLINESS   < ...... / 10 >

WEIRDNESS   < ...... / 10 >

FUN FACTOR   < ...... / 10 >

NAME

LIVES IN

WORKS AT

WAS BORN IN

GREW UP IN

FAVOURITE HOBBIES

FAVOURITE FOOD

BEST PRESENT GIVEN

SPENDS A LOT OF TIME THINKING ABOUT

FRIENDLINESS   < ...... / 10 >

WEIRDNESS   < ...... / 10 >

FUN FACTOR   < ...... / 10 >

WEIRD-O-METRE

Mum / Dad

SUMMARY

I MUST FIND OUT MORE ABOUT   ....

I WANT TO TRY AND AVOID   ....

SOCIAL MEDIA

	FACEBOOK	TWITTER	TUMBLR	INSTAGRAM	PINTEREST	LINKEDIN
WEEK 1 HOW MANY FRIENDS/ FOLLOWERS?						
WEEK 2 HOW MANY FRIENDS/ FOLLOWERS?						
WEEK 3 HOW MANY FRIENDS/ FOLLOWERS?						
WEEK 4 HOW MANY FRIENDS/ FOLLOWERS?						

NOW FILL IN THE HIGHEST AND LOWEST NUMBERS ON THE Y AXIS OF THIS GRAPH, AND USE IT TO PLOT THESE RESULTS AND SEE WHICH IS GROWING FASTEST!

FACEBOOK ☐
TWITTER ☐

TUMBLR ☐
INSTAGRAM ☐

PINTEREST ☐
LINKEDIN ☐

CHOOSE A COLOUR FOR EACH ONE.

	WEEK 1	WEEK 2	WEEK 3	WEEK 4

3

ARE YOU HOOKED ON TWITTER OR ADDICTED TO FACEBOOK? TRY AND GET A HANDLE ON YOUR SOCIAL MEDIA USE HERE!

NEXT TIME YOU HAVE A REALLY GOOD PICTURE TO POST, TRY IT ACROSS ALL YOUR PLATFORMS AND RECORD THE RESULTS HERE!

FACEBOOK LIKES	....
SHARES	....
COMMENTS	....
TWITTER LIKES	....
RETWEETS	....
REPLYS	....
TUMBLR LIKES	....
REBLOGS	....
COMMENTS	....

INSTAGRAM LIKES	....
SHARES	....
COMMENTS	....
PINTEREST LIKES	....
PINS	....
COMMENTS	....
LINKEDIN	
ARE YOU KIDDING? THIS IS	
NOT HOW LINKEDIN WORKS.	

NOW KEEP A TALLY OF HOW MANY TIMES A DAY YOU CHECK IN WITH THOSE SOCIAL NETWORKS!

	MONDAY	TUESDAY	WEDNESDAY	THURSDAY	FRIDAY	SATURDAY	SUNDAY	TOTAL
FACEBOOK								
TWITTER								
TUMBLR								
INSTAGRAM								
PINTEREST								
LINKEDIN								

SUMMARY

THE SOCIAL MEDIA I USE MOST IS ....

MY FASTEST GROWING ACCOUNT IS ....

I NEED TO SPEND LESS TIME ON ....

I SHOULD REALLY LOOK INTO USING MORE OF ....

AT THE MOVIES

MOVIES I HAVE WATCHED

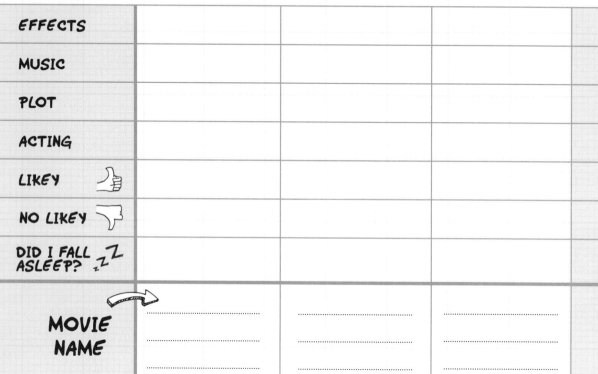

EFFECTS			
MUSIC			
PLOT			
ACTING			
LIKEY 👍			
NO LIKEY 👎			
DID I FALL ASLEEP? zᶻᶻ			
MOVIE NAME	....	....	....

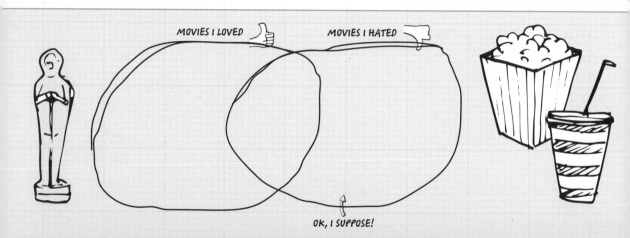

MOVIES I LOVED 👍   MOVIES I HATED 👎

OK, I SUPPOSE!

LABEL AND RATE THE MOVIES YOU'VE SEEN (MARK FROM 1-5 STARS!)

MOVIES I HAVE WATCHED

EFFECTS			
MUSIC			
PLOT			
ACTING			
LIKEY 👍			
NO LIKEY 👎			
DID I FALL ASLEEP? zZ			
MOVIE NAME	....	....	....

SUMMARY

 I TOTALLY LOVED [ ] 5-STAR MOVIES

 I NEARLY DIED OF BOREDOM WATCHING [ ] 1-STAR MOVIES

CULTURAL COUCH POTATOES

EVERY TIME YOU STREAM MUSIC, MOVIES OR TV THIS WEEK, WRITE DOWN HOW MANY
HOURS YOU STREAMED FOR IN THIS CHART. THEN TURN THE TOTALS INTO PERCENTAGES,
AND FILL IN THE PIE CHART BELOW TO DISPLAY YOUR RESULTS.

	MONDAY	TUESDAY	WEDNESDAY	THURSDAY	FRIDAY	SATURDAY	SUNDAY	TOTAL
MUSIC								
MOVIES								
TV SHOWS								

GRAND TOTAL OF HOURS STREAMED

MUSIC ☐
MOVIES ☐
TV SHOWS ☐

SUMMARY

I AM SHOCKED AT HOW MUCH TIME I SPEND STREAMING ....

....

I DEFINITELY DON'T SPEND ENOUGH TIME STREAMING ....

....

THESE DAYS, THERE'S NO NEED TO LEAVE THE HOUSE IF YOU WANT TO WATCH SOMETHING GOOD! TRACK YOUR STREAMING HABITS HERE!

USE OUR HANDY CHART TO RATE EACH INDIVIDUAL EPISODE OF WHATEVER TV SHOWS YOU'RE BINGE-WATCHING AT THE MOMENT!

SERIES NAME & EPISODE NUMBER	STAR RATING OUT OF 5	SERIES NAME & EPISODE NUMBER	STAR RATING OUT OF 5	SERIES NAME & EPISODE NUMBER	STAR RATING OUT OF 5

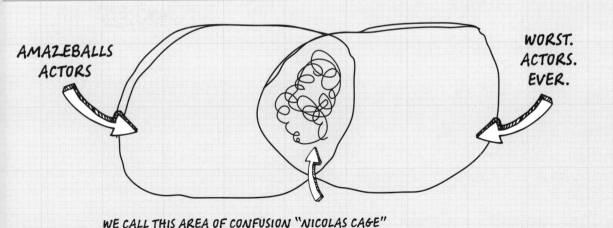

AMAZEBALLS ACTORS

WORST. ACTORS. EVER.

WE CALL THIS AREA OF CONFUSION "NICOLAS CAGE"

STUCK IN A BOOK

BOOK TITLE	NUMBER OF PAGES	RATING (OUT OF 5 STARS)

BOOKS, MAGAZINES, JOURNALS – WHAT DO YOU READ WHEN YOU HAVE THE TIME? KEEP AN EYE ON YOUR READING HABITS ON THIS PAGE!

BOOKS I WANT TO READ

AUTHORS I WANT TO MEET

MAGAZINES I WANT TO SUBSCRIBE TO

BOOKS I HATE ABSOLUTELY

CHARACTERS I AM IN LOVE WITH

BOOKS I WISH I'D WRITTEN

SUMMARY

TOTAL NUMBER OF BOOKS I READ THIS YEAR ....

TOTAL NUMBER OF PAGES I READ THIS YEAR ....

MY FAVOURITE BOOK THIS YEAR WAS ....

MY LEAST FAVOURITE BOOK THIS YEAR WAS ....

THE NEXT BOOK I WANT TO READ IS ....

CHECK OUT THE CLASSICS

	RATING OUT OF 5		RATING OUT OF 5		RATING OUT OF 5
CITIZEN KANE		SOME LIKE IT HOT		GROUNDHOG DAY	
THE GODFATHER		THE WIZARD OF OZ		CLOSE ENCOUNTERS OF THE THIRD KIND	
VERTIGO		STAR WARS		THELMA & LOUISE	
2001: A SPACE ODYSSEY		JAWS		RAIDERS OF THE LOST ARK	
SINGIN' IN THE RAIN		DR STRANGELOVE		BRINGING UP BABY	
PSYCHO		IT'S A WONDERFUL LIFE		APOCALYPSE NOW	
CASABLANCA		SUNSET BOULEVARD		ET: THE EXTRA-TERRESTRIAL	
NORTH BY NORTHWEST		THE THIRD MAN		12 YEARS A SLAVE	
GOODFELLAS		BRIEF ENCOUNTER			
THE APARTMENT		THE GRADUATE			
PULP FICTION		BACK TO THE FUTURE			

MOVIES I LIKE

MOVIES MY MUM LIKES

THESE ONES ARE PROBABLY CLASSICS

HOW MANY OF THESE CLASSIC MOVIES AND BOOKS HAVE YOU SEEN AND READ? AND WHICH ONES DID YOU LIKE THE BEST?

	RATING OUT OF 5		RATING OUT OF 5		RATING OUT OF 5
ROBINSON CRUSOE BY DANIEL DEFOE		**THE LION, THE WITCH, AND THE WARDROBE (CHRONICLES OF NARNIA, #1)** BY C.S. LEWIS		**ONE FLEW OVER THE CUCKOO'S NEST** BY KEN KESEY	
GULLIVER'S TRAVELS BY JONATHAN SWIFT		**LORD OF THE FLIES** BY WILLIAM GOLDING		**A CLOCKWORK ORANGE** BY ANTHONY BURGESS	
FRANKENSTEIN BY MARY SHELLEY		**ANIMAL FARM** BY GEORGE ORWELL		**WATCHMEN** BY ALAN MOORE	
PRIDE AND PREJUDICE BY JANE AUSTEN		**CATCH-22** BY JOSEPH HELLER		**NEVER LET ME GO** BY KAZUO ISHIGURO	
DON QUIXOTE BY MIGUEL DE CERVANTES		**JANE EYRE** BY CHARLOTTE BRONTË		**ATONEMENT** BY IAN MCEWAN	
TO KILL A MOCKINGBIRD BY HARPER LEE		**THE GRAPES OF WRATH** BY JOHN STEINBECK		**THINGS FALL APART** BY CHINUA ACHEBE	
1984 BY GEORGE ORWELL		**GONE WITH THE WIND** BY MARGARET MITCHELL		**MRS. DALLOWAY** BY VIRGINIA WOOLF	
THE LORD OF THE RINGS BY J.R.R. TOLKIEN		**SLAUGHTERHOUSE-FIVE** BY KURT VONNEGUT		**WUTHERING HEIGHTS** BY EMILY BRONTË	
THE CATCHER IN THE RYE BY J.D. SALINGER		**BELOVED** BY TONI MORRISON		**ONE HUNDRED YEARS OF SOLITUDE** BY GABRIEL GARCÍA MÁRQUEZ	
THE GREAT GATSBY BY F. SCOTT FITZGERALD		**LOLITA** BY VLADIMIR NABOKOV		**THE CAIRO TRILOGY** BY NAGUIB MAHFOUZ	

SUMMARY

I HAVE WATCHED .... CLASSIC MOVIES.

I HAVE READ .... CLASSIC NOVELS.

I DON'T UNDERSTAND WHY HARRY POTTER / TWILIGHT / HUNGER GAMES* ARE NOT ON BOTH OF THESE LISTS. (*PLEASE DELETE AS APPLICABLE.)

IN THE COUNTRY

TICK OFF EVERY DAY YOU GO FOR A 30 MINUTE WALK THIS MONTH.

1	2	3	4	5	6	7	8	9	10	11	12	13	14	15	16	17	18	19	20	21	22	23	24	25	26	27	28	29	30	

WRITE DOWN YOUR FAVOURITE PLACES TO WALK NEARBY

....

....

....

THESE DAYS IT'S EASY TO GET STUCK INDOORS. WHEN WAS THE LAST TIME YOU WENT FOR A WALK TO SMELL THE ROSES?!

OF COURSE, IT'S PRETTY EASY TO BRING THE GREEN STUFF INTO YOUR HOME TOO, EVEN IF YOU DON'T HAVE A GARDEN.

MAKING A WINDOW GARDEN

PICK A WINDOWSILL THAT GETS LOTS OF SUN ☐
CLEAN THE WINDOWSILL ☐
FIND A PLASTIC TRAY TO HOLD YOUR PLANTS ☐
CHOOSE SOME POTS (OR OLD TINS AND JARS) ☐
PUT IN A HEAVY LAYER (E.G. STONES) FOR STABILITY ☐
FILL UP WITH SPECIAL COMPOST MADE FOR CONTAINERS ☐

PLANT SEEDS IN THE MIDDLE ☐
KEEP THE SOIL FEELING MOIST ☐
ADD EXTRA LIQUID FEED EVERY TWO WEEKS ☐
WATCH THEM GROW! ☐

AS LONG AS YOU FIND A SUNNY SPOT, THESE HERBS SHOULD THRIVE INDOORS AND MAKE YOUR COOKING MORE FRESH AND FRAGRANT!

HERB GARDEN

CHIVES ☐
MINT ☐
PARSLEY ☐
OREGANO ☐
SAGE ☐
BAY

THYME ☐
ROSEMARY ☐
BASIL ☐
CORIANDER ☐
GINGER ☐

GET BIRDS ON YOUR WINDOWSILL!

CHOOSE A WINDOW CATS CANNOT ACCESS! ☐
DISGUISE THE WINDOW WITH A THIN CURTAIN, SO BIRDS AREN'T SCARED BY MOVEMENT INDOORS. ☐
FILL A SAUCER WITH WATER TO ACT AS A BIRD BATH. ☐

PROVIDE SOME SHELTER – A SMALL BOX OR PLANTS. ☐
ADD A BIRD FEEDER AND KEEP IT TOPPED UP. ☐
ENJOY THE BEAUTIFUL WILDLIFE AT YOUR WINDOW! ☐

MOOD JOURNAL

ASSIGN A COLOUR TO EACH OF THESE MOODS, THEN COLOUR
EACH DAY'S SQUARE USING THE RIGHT PROPORTION OF MOODS.

	DATE	DATE	DATE	DATE	DATE
SUNDAY					
SATURDAY					
FRIDAY					
THURSDAY					
WEDNESDAY					
TUESDAY					
MONDAY					

HAPPY MEMORIES

SAD MEMORIES

BITTERSWEET MEMORIES

TRACK YOUR MOODS AND HOW THEY FLUCTUATE EACH DAY. AT THE END OF EACH DAY, WRITE DOWN HOW YOU FELT.

HAPPY ☐	ANGRY ☐	STRESSED ☐
SAD ☐	ANXIOUS ☐	EXCITED ☐

☐ ....

☐ ....

	DATE	DATE	DATE	DATE	DATE ....
SUNDAY					
SATURDAY					
FRIDAY					
THURSDAY					
WEDNESDAY					
TUESDAY					
MONDAY					

SUMMARY

I SPEND A LOT OF TIME FEELING ....

I WANT TO CHANGE HOW MUCH TIME I SPEND FEELING ....

I WANT TO SPEND MORE TIME FEELING ....

PERSON TO PERSONALITY

ALLOT A PERCENTAGE TO EACH OF THESE PERSONALITY TRAITS FOR EACH PERSON.
(AND MAKE SURE EACH ONE ADDS UP TO 100%!) THEN YOU CAN COMPARE AND CONTRAST!

ME

NAME ....
ANXIOUS ....
PESSIMISTIC ....
EXCITABLE ....
IMPULSIVE ....
SOCIABLE ....
LIVELY ....
CALM ....
THOUGHTFUL ....
TOTAL = 100%
MOSTLY = ...

MUM

NAME ....
ANXIOUS ....
PESSIMISTIC ....
EXCITABLE ....
IMPULSIVE ....
SOCIABLE ....
LIVELY ....
CALM ....
THOUGHTFUL ....
TOTAL = 100%
MOSTLY = ...

DAD

NAME ....
ANXIOUS ....
PESSIMISTIC ....
EXCITABLE ....
IMPULSIVE ....
SOCIABLE ....
LIVELY ....
CALM ....
THOUGHTFUL ....
TOTAL = 100%
MOSTLY = ...

NAME ....
ANXIOUS ....
PESSIMISTIC ....
EXCITABLE ....
IMPULSIVE ....
SOCIABLE ....
LIVELY ....
CALM ....
THOUGHTFUL ....
TOTAL = 100%
MOSTLY = ...

IF YOU'RE MOSTLY **ANXIOUS AND PESSIMISTIC**, YOU'RE **MELANCHOLIC**

IF YOU'RE MOSTLY **EXCITABLE AND IMPULSIVE**, YOU'RE **CHOLERIC**

IF YOU'RE MOSTLY **SOCIABLE AND LIVELY**, YOU'RE **SANGUINE**

IF YOU'RE MOSTLY **CALM AND THOUGHTFUL**, YOU'RE **PHLEGMATIC**

FROM EYSENCK AND EYSENK, PERSONALITY AND INDIVIDUAL DIFFERENCES (PLENUM PUBLISHING, 1958)

EVER WONDERED HOW SIMILAR YOU ARE TO YOUR FRIENDS AND FAMILY?
USE THESE CHARTS TO COMPARE AND CONTRAST YOUR PERSONALITIES!

Chart 1

NAME ....
ANXIOUS ....
PESSIMISTIC ....
EXCITABLE ....
IMPULSIVE ....
SOCIABLE ....
LIVELY ....
CALM ....
THOUGHTFUL ....
TOTAL = 100%
MOSTLY = ...

Chart 2

NAME ....
ANXIOUS ....
PESSIMISTIC ....
EXCITABLE ....
IMPULSIVE ....
SOCIABLE ....
LIVELY ....
CALM ....
THOUGHTFUL ....
TOTAL = 100%
MOSTLY = ...

Chart 3

NAME ....
ANXIOUS ....
PESSIMISTIC ....
EXCITABLE ....
IMPULSIVE ....
SOCIABLE ....
LIVELY ....
CALM ....
THOUGHTFUL ....
TOTAL = 100%
MOSTLY = ...

Chart 4

NAME ....
ANXIOUS ....
PESSIMISTIC ....
EXCITABLE ....
IMPULSIVE ....
SOCIABLE ....
LIVELY ....
CALM ....
THOUGHTFUL ....
TOTAL = 100%
MOSTLY = ...

SUMMARY

I AM MOSTLY ....

I SHARE THESE TRAITS WITH ....

I AM SURPRISED HOW MANY OF MY FRIENDS ARE ....

I GUESS I SHOULD WORK ON MY ....

LAZY WEEKEND DECISIONS

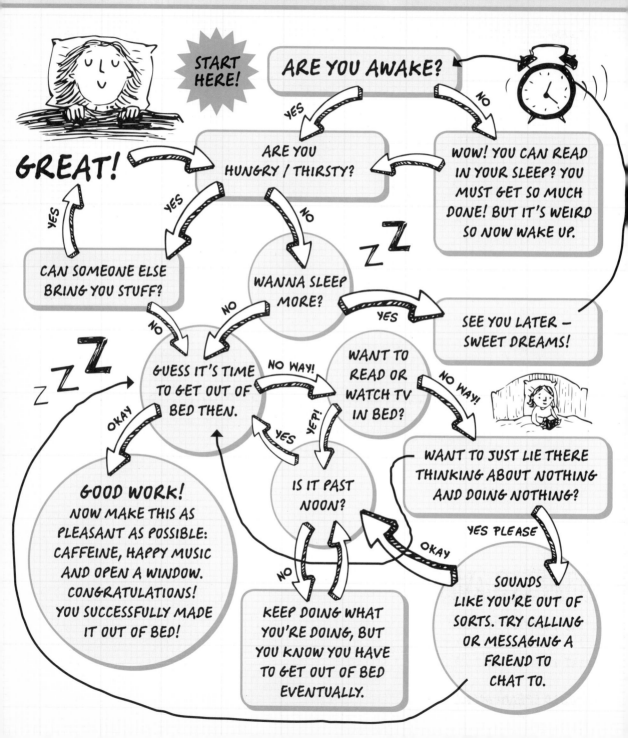

IT'S HARD TO GET STARTED AT WEEKENDS SOMETIMES. IT'S HARD TO GET OUT OF BED SOMETIMES. USE THIS CHART TO FIGURE OUT HOW TO SPEND YOUR LAZY SATURDAY MORNINGS...

LAZING AT WEEKENDS IS IMPORTANT. MARK OFF BELOW EVERY DAY YOU HAD A LIE-IN.

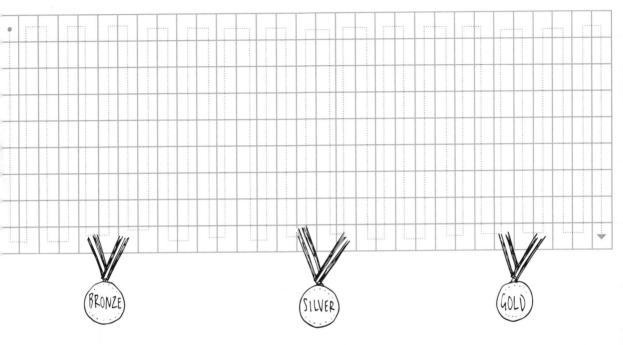

BRONZE

SILVER

GOLD

TICK OFF ALL THE THINGS YOU'RE _NOT_ GOING TO DO ON A LAZY WEEKEND.

EXERCISE ☐   EAT HEALTHILY ☐   ORGANISE ANYTHING ☐

SEE FAMILY ☐   MEDITATE ☐   CLEAN ANYTHING ☐

DO LAUNDRY ☐   SEE DAYLIGHT ☐   ANYTHING ☐

SUMMARY

WHAT I LIKE MOST ABOUT WEEKENDS IS ....

WHAT I HATE MOST ABOUT WEEKENDS IS ....

I SHOULD SPEND MORE TIME AT WEEKENDS ....

SKILLS AND HOBBIES

SPORTS	READING	PLAYING GAMES	PLAYING AN INSTRUMENT	LISTENING TO MUSIC	TAKING PHOTOS	WRITING	DRAWING	WATCHING TV	MAKING PARODY TWITTER ACCOUNTS

SUMMARY

I NEED TO DO MORE ....

I NEED TO DO LESS ....

FILL IN A BLOCK EACH TIME YOU DO ONE OF THESE ACTIVITIES, THEN USE THE OPPOSITE SIDE TO PLAN OUT NEW ONES, WHETHER YOU WANT TO BETTER YOURSELF OR ARE ALL ABOUT THE FUN!

READ...

~~READ "MY LIFE IN DIAGRAMS"~~

AN AMERICAN NOVEL

A FRENCH NOVEL

THE TV GUIDE

WAR AND PEACE

A POEM

LEARN...

~~ENGLISH~~

FRENCH

SPANISH

ITALIAN

JAPANESE

TIME TO LEARN...	TYPE	DATE I WILL START THIS
NEW LANGUAGE		
NEW SOFTWARE		
NEW SPORT		
NEW GAME		
NEW RECIPE		
....		
....		

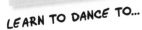

LEARN TO PLAY...

~~TENNIS~~

FOOTBALL

BASEBALL

BASKETBALL

CHESS-BOXING

LEARN TO DANCE TO...

~~BEYONCÉ~~

SWING MUSIC

LITTLE RICHARD

WATCH ME (WHIP / NAE NAE)

BAGPIPES

ONE DAY AT A TIME

EXAMPLE

	MONDAY	TUESDAY	WEDNESDAY	THURSDAY	FRIDAY	SATURDAY	SUNDAY
~~WAKE UP~~							
~~READ THIS~~							
CROSS THIS OUT							
AND THIS							
WEAR CLOTHES							
EAT JUNK FOOD							
DRINK LIQUIDS							
NAP							
PRETEND TO DO SOMETHING							
SECOND NAP							

	MONDAY	TUESDAY	WEDNESDAY	THURSDAY	FRIDAY	SATURDAY	SUNDAY

SUPPLIES NEEDED FOR FURTHER LIST-MAKING

- PAPER ☐
- PENS ☐

WORDS THAT SOUND LIKE LIST:
GIST, MIST, FIST WRIST, KISSED

OF COURSE, SOME DAYS ARE HARDER THAN OTHERS, AND SOMETIMES YOU JUST NEED TO TAKE THINGS ONE STEP AT A TIME. USE THIS PAGE TO MAKE YOURSELF (ACHIEVABLE) DAILY TO-DO LISTS!

	MONDAY	TUESDAY	WEDNESDAY	THURSDAY	FRIDAY	SATURDAY	SUNDAY

	MONDAY	TUESDAY	WEDNESDAY	THURSDAY	FRIDAY	SATURDAY	SUNDAY

SUMMARY

I FAILED TO GET DRESSED ON .... DAYS.

I SUCCESSFULLY FED MYSELF ON .... DAYS.

I FAILED TO COMPLETE TO-DO LISTS ON .... DAYS.

I SUCCESSFULLY COMPLETED TO-DO LISTS ON .... DAYS.

WORK-LIFE BALANCE

SLEEPING ☐   SOCIALISING ☐

EATING ☐   CHORES ☐

GROOMING ☐   RELAXING ☐

TRAVELLING ☐   OTHER ☐

WORKING ☐

ASSIGN COLOURS TO THE KEY AND COLOUR IN BLOCKS ACCORDING TO HOW YOU SPEND YOUR TIME EACH DAY.

	MONDAY	TUESDAY	WEDNESDAY	THURSDAY	FRIDAY	SATURDAY	SUNDAY
PM							
AM							

IT'S ALL ABOUT GETTING THE RIGHT WORK-LIFE BALANCE, AND HOW BETTER TO FIGURE IT OUT THAN BY LOOKING AT EVERY ASPECT OF YOUR DAY IN DETAIL!

COUNT UP HOW MANY BLOCKS YOU COLOURED IN FOR EACH DAY AND RECORD HOW IT ALL ADDS UP HERE.

MONDAY — TOTAL HOURS SPENT

- SLEEPING
- EATING
- GROOMING
- TRAVELLING
- WORKING
- SOCIALISING
- CHORES
- RELAXING
- OTHER

TUESDAY — TOTAL HOURS SPENT

- SLEEPING
- EATING
- GROOMING
- TRAVELLING
- WORKING
- SOCIALISING
- CHORES
- RELAXING
- OTHER

WEDNESDAY — TOTAL HOURS SPENT

- SLEEPING
- EATING
- GROOMING
- TRAVELLING
- WORKING
- SOCIALISING
- CHORES
- RELAXING
- OTHER

THURSDAY — TOTAL HOURS SPENT

- SLEEPING
- EATING
- GROOMING
- TRAVELLING
- WORKING
- SOCIALISING
- CHORES
- RELAXING
- OTHER

FRIDAY — TOTAL HOURS SPENT

- SLEEPING
- EATING
- GROOMING
- TRAVELLING
- WORKING
- SOCIALISING
- CHORES
- RELAXING
- OTHER

SATURDAY — TOTAL HOURS SPENT

- SLEEPING
- EATING
- GROOMING
- TRAVELLING
- WORKING
- SOCIALISING
- CHORES
- RELAXING
- OTHER

SUNDAY — TOTAL HOURS SPENT

- SLEEPING
- EATING
- GROOMING
- TRAVELLING
- WORKING
- SOCIALISING
- CHORES
- RELAXING
- OTHER

TOTAL HOURS PER WEEK

- SLEEPING
- EATING
- GROOMING
- TRAVELLING
- WORKING
- SOCIALISING
- CHORES
- RELAXING
- OTHER

GRAND TOTAL

SUMMARY

*DELETE AS APPLICABLE

I SLEEP TOO MUCH / NOT ENOUGH / EXACTLY THE RIGHT AMOUNT.*

I EAT TOO MUCH / NOT ENOUGH / EXACTLY THE RIGHT AMOUNT.*

I RELAX TOO MUCH / NOT ENOUGH / EXACTLY THE RIGHT AMOUNT.*

I SOCIALISE TOO MUCH / NOT ENOUGH / EXACTLY THE RIGHT AMOUNT.*

LIVE THE LIFE YOU WANT

FAMILY
WHAT DO YOU WANT FROM YOUR FAMILY LIFE?

CAREER
WHAT DO YOU WANT TO ACHIEVE?

FINANCIAL
WHAT DO YOU WANT AND HOW CAN YOU GET IT?

EDUCATION
WHAT DO YOU NEED TO HELP YOU ACHIEVE OTHER GOALS?

ARTISTIC
DO YOU HAVE ANY ARTISTIC GOALS YOU WANT TO SET?

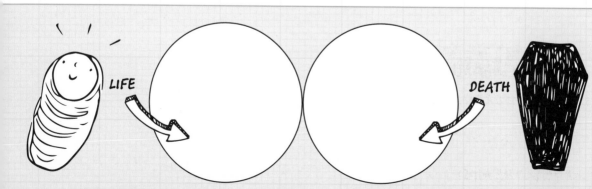

LIFE

DEATH

ATTITUDE
IS THERE ANYTHING ABOUT YOURSELF YOU WANT TO CHANGE?

PHYSICAL
IS THERE ANYTHING PHYSICAL YOU WANT TO CHANGE?

FUN
THERE'S MORE TO LIFE THAN MONEY! WHAT ELSE DO YOU WANT TO EXPERIENCE?

FRIENDSHIPS
HOW DO YOU WANT YOUR FRIENDSHIPS TO DEVELOP?

THE WORLD BEYOND
HOW CAN YOU MAKE THE WORLD A BETTER PLACE?

SUMMARY

THE LEAST IMPORTANT GOAL RIGHT NOW IS ....

THIS YEAR THE MOST IMPORTANT GOAL TO FOCUS ON IS ....

NEXT YEAR THE MOST IMPORTANT GOAL WILL BE ....

ON THE TOWN

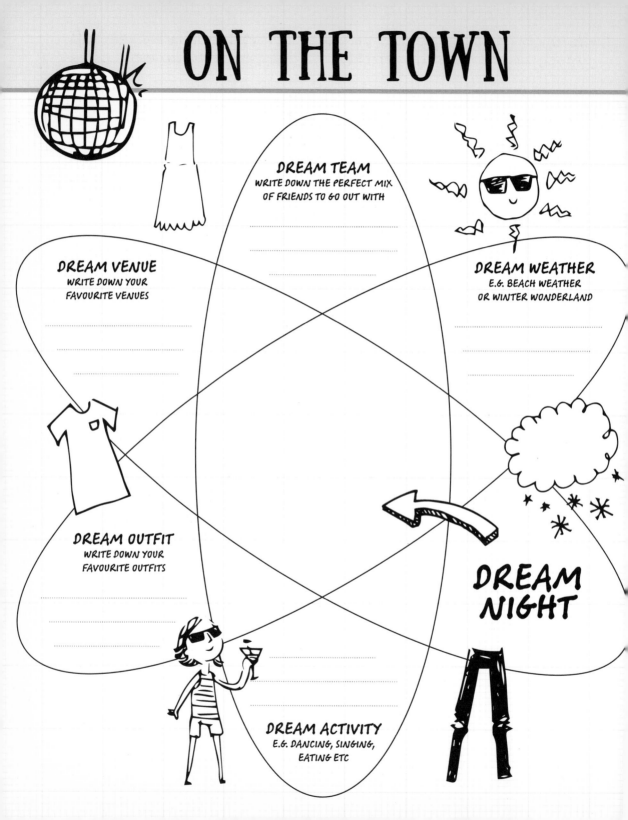

DREAM TEAM
WRITE DOWN THE PERFECT MIX
OF FRIENDS TO GO OUT WITH

DREAM VENUE
WRITE DOWN YOUR
FAVOURITE VENUES

DREAM WEATHER
E.G. BEACH WEATHER
OR WINTER WONDERLAND

DREAM OUTFIT
WRITE DOWN YOUR
FAVOURITE OUTFITS

**DREAM
NIGHT**

DREAM ACTIVITY
E.G. DANCING, SINGING,
EATING ETC

TIME TO RELAX! USE THIS PAGE TO PLAN YOUR PERFECT EVENING OUT AND MAKE SURE NOTHING GOES WRONG ON THE NIGHT!

CHECKLIST!

ALL THE BORING STUFF YOUR MUM WOULD WANT TO KNOW

HOW ARE YOU GOING TO GET THERE? ☐

HOW ARE YOU GOING TO GET BACK? ☐

HAVE YOU BOOKED TRANSPORT? ☐

DO YOU NEED A DESIGNATED DRIVER? ☐

HAVE YOU BOOKED THE PLACE? ☐

HOW MUCH MONEY DO YOU NEED? ☐

IS YOUR PHONE CHARGED? ☐

ARE YOU GOING TO BE WARM ENOUGH? ☐

CHECKLIST!

ALL THE IMPORTANT STUFF

ARE MY FRIENDS GOING TO UPSTAGE ME? ☐

WHO LOOKS BEST? ☐

ARE THERE ANY FIGHTS BREWING? ☐

HOW AMAZING ARE THESE SHOES? ☐

ARE MY SELFIES GOING TO LOOK OKAY? ☐

NIGHT OUT

FUN	____ / (OUT OF 10)	____ / (OUT OF 10)
DRAMA	____ / (OUT OF 10)	____ / (OUT OF 10)
SUCCESS	____ / (OUT OF 10)	____ / (OUT OF 10)

TREAT YOURSELF!

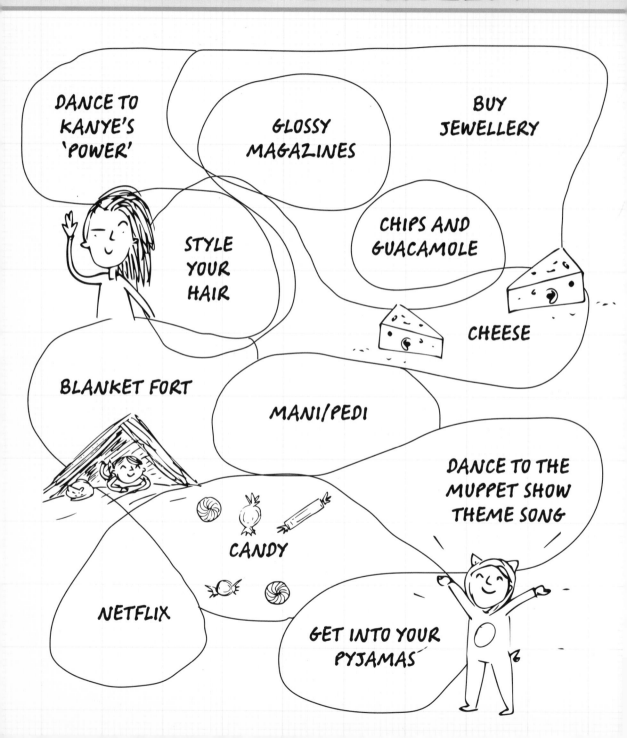

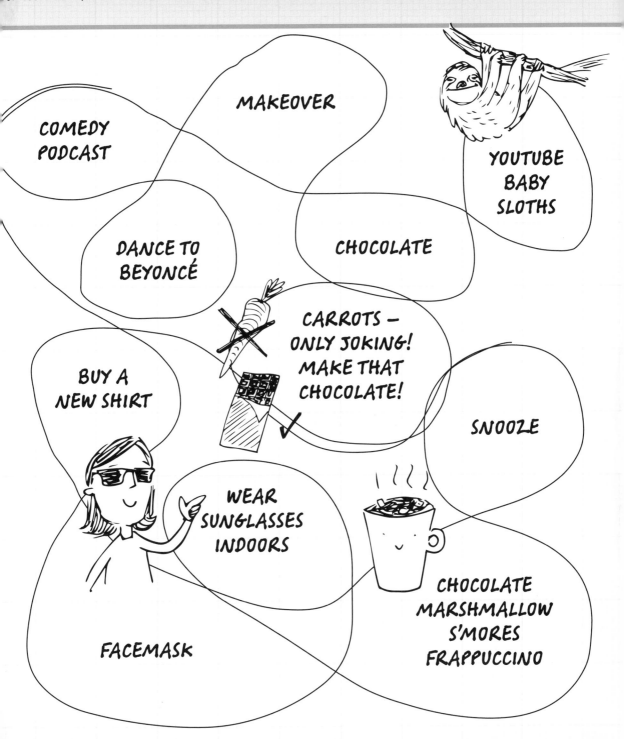